I0671911

DISPLAY

Display

Written by Nicolaas A Gad

Copyright © 2026 by Nicolaas A Gad

All rights reserved.

This is a work of fiction. Names, characters, places, and events are either the product of the author's imagination or are used fictitiously. Any resemblance to actual persons, living or dead, or to actual events is purely coincidental.

No part of this book may be reproduced, distributed, or transmitted in any form or by any means, including photocopying, recording, or other electronic or mechanical methods, without the prior written permission of the publisher, except in the case of brief quotations embodied in critical reviews and certain other non-commercial uses permitted by copyright law. For permission requests, contact the publisher.

Self-published by

Nicolaas A Gad

albertgad67@gmail.com

ISBN: 978-1-7637114-4-0

First Edition: 2026

Cover design by Nicolaas A Gad

Printed in Australia

Author's Note

This book is a work of fiction. While it draws on psychological, philosophical, and experiential themes that may feel realistic, all characters, events, and circumstances are fictionalised and created for narrative purposes.

The story does not intend to promote or instruct the use of drugs or risky behaviour.

Any depictions of altered states, decision-making, or consequences are presented within a fictional context and should not be interpreted as medical, legal, or lifestyle guidance.

Any references to substances, dosages, or methods reflect the character's subjective and often misguided understanding and should not be interpreted as guidance.

Reader discretion is advised.

Some depictions are intentionally exaggerated or compressed for narrative effect.

TABLE OF CONTENTS

ONE

I arrived at my friends' once again for another weekend of who knows what ahead. I knocked and waited. It wasn't too late yet, and the sun was still well above the horizon, but those of us who worked had finished for the day. I could hear chatter through the door, and the smell of marijuana seeped to the outside where I stood. The door handle turned, clicked unlocked, and I was invited inside.

As I walked in, I placed my things in the kitchen adjacent to the front door. I poured myself a glass of water, and walked down the hallway, towards the talking in the living room.

I'd brought with me one hundred dollars. That was all I ever had left for the weekend, but for what I had come here for, it was plenty.

'How would I split it?' I asked myself. A packet of cigarettes was a given, which was about thirty dollars at the time. I would also need a couple of grams of weed, which was another thirty dollars. If there was some around, I'd get some MDMA as well, which was another twenty dollars.

That was eighty dollars in total, which only left twenty dollars for food for the entire weekend, but I didn't tend to think of that, only what drugs I wanted to consume. I was sure I would find something in my friend's fridge anyway, even if it was just some bread and sauce - a 'sauce sandwich' I called it.

As I made my way into the living room at the end of the hall, an acquaintance greeted me. We weren't very close, and we mostly knew each other from Friday nights hanging out there.

"What're you doing this weekend?" Ashon asked.

"Just weed probably, maybe some M, you?" I replied. His eyebrows raised.

"Just catching up with some mates, fishing tomorrow," he said in a tone that implied I'd misinterpreted his question.

'Why did I say what drugs I was doing?' I thought to myself, feeling a bit self-conscious about my response, and realising stating what drugs I was doing to that question wasn't normal.

I'd given him a glimpse into how my mind worked, and how it and my experience was entirely framed around drugs. It was the first thing I thought of, and I was so absorbed into this way of thinking I didn't question it. It was only when Ashon unknowingly broke my pattern of thinking with his concerned look that I realised.

I found a seat. There was a mix going around the table. A mix is what we would call chopped up marijuana mixed with tobacco, that we would smoke out of a bong (a type of glass pipe with water in it to filter the smoke). 'Perfect,' I thought, looking forward to taking my first hit.

We smoked for a few hours, talking, listening to music, and watching videos on the TV. I always found I was very sociable before I smoked weed, but after my first few inhales my anxiety increased, especially if there were people around that I wasn't so familiar with.

I talked less, listened more, and was self-conscious of how I sat, spoke, walked and moved, as if all eyes were intensely focussed on me, waiting to find something to judge me for. But despite my uncomfortability, I still smoked, enjoying the dopamine hit that came right after inhaling, and the escape it provided from my everyday life.

It was usually this anxiety and introversion the weed induced that encouraged me to seek out other drugs, especially MDMA, also known as ecstasy.

I got up from my seat and went to my friend's room, Caleb, who was one of the two people that actually lived in this house, and asked if he had any. This question's answer would determine my night, and my mind teetered on a crossroads of possibilities. To my left in my mind I could see an excitement filled night of socialisation and good feelings, and to my right, a hazy night of smoking weed and falling asleep early on the lounge. The anticipation weighed on me.

He said yes... "Twenty five for one, or two for forty."

Of course I opted for two.

Just as my purchase was complete and I placed the small ziplock bag he gave me into my wallet, I heard the front door open. James was home.

James also lived in the house. He shared it with the friend I'd just bought drugs off. James worked at a pharmacy, and had knowledge of most drugs, including obscure ones you could buy over the counter without a prescription. He always informed us of what we were taking, dosages, safety information, and he was the person who regularly introduced us to new ways of getting high.

"Hey man," I said, excited to see him, reaching out my hand to shake his.

"Good to see you bro," he replied with a smile, "just going to get myself sorted and I'll be right with you."

After he had a shower, changed his clothes, and got settled, we sat in the lounge to smoke and catch up.

"I got this today," James said, reaching into his bag and pulling out three bottles of what appeared to be kids cough medicine.

"Painstop night. Have you ever heard of it?" He asked me. I hadn't, and shook my head.

He explained it was a mixture of codeine, an opiate pain killer often used to suppress coughing, and promethazine, an antihistamine that made you drowsy and potentiated the effects of the codeine.

Up until this point, I'd never dabbled with painkillers. I'd heard they were very addictive, and after some research on my phone, I learned that codeine was in the same class of drugs as heroin, albeit much weaker and incomparable in its reputation.

"How does it make you feel?" I questioned, curious about what effect this would have on my consciousness.

I always found it fascinating after discovering drugs how consciousness could be altered in so many different ways beyond alcohol's effects. This opened up a world of possibilities inside of my mind to explore. I always perceived it as travelling, and it felt like I was discovering the colour spectrum of the mind.

"It's calming, like floating, you just feel chill. But you have to be careful mixing it with things like alcohol," he explained, "as it slows your breathing, and mixing downers can be dangerous." A downer was a drug that made you feel slower and more relaxed, as opposed to an upper, which would give you energy and speed you up.

He reached into his bag again, this time pulling out a bottle of lemonade to mix the cough medicine with.

'What a concoction we have tonight,' I thought to myself. 'So many options.'

I walked up the hallway to the kitchen to fetch three cups. I filled them with ice from the freezer and returned to the lounge room, excited to add to my already altered state.

First, the painstop was carefully poured into the cups by James. It was a purple colour, and slightly thick and syrupy. An equal amount each was measured; we started with what we thought was an entry level dose to test the effects. The syrup filled to a few centimetres above the bottom of each cup.

Next, the lemonade was added, sizzling with a satisfactory sound as it blended with the purple syrup to make an appetising looking drink.

"Cheers," we all said, each taking our cups, and tasting this new drug.

It was just the three of us drinking it - James, Caleb, and I - and so I suppose it was the three of us going on this journey together.

It tasted nice, the lemonade turning a usually syrupy and intensely berry flavoured medicine into an enjoyable sparkling drink. It was nice to sit, sip and talk, much like having an alcoholic beverage in our hands, or puffing on a cigarette while chatting. It was comforting knowing that what we had to accompany our conversation was something that would slowly accompany our minds as well.

Minute by minute, we felt more relaxed, our eyes felt heavier, and the seats we were on were feeling comfier. I remember at about thirty minutes, I had already begun to love the drug, concreting it in my mind as something more favoured than alcohol. It felt cleaner, less messy, and more comfortable. I felt coherent yet tranquil, and complemented with marijuana, it was an almost perfect combination of bliss and cognitive alteration. I can only describe it as a feeling of floating cognitive enhancement.

At about nine o'clock, when the night still felt early, and the day felt truly over, I was considering my next move. The conversation was still active and smoothly continuing around ideas about our future, and a great appreciation for the lives we had already.
"It's getting harder to keep my eyes open," I mentioned to the others.

"Yeah, and we still have two bottles left... I'm pretty keen to keep this night going. It's been good so far," James said.

Caleb agreed.

I reached into my pocket to retrieve my wallet.

"Hey James, do you know anything about mixing this with..." I didn't want to actually say it, but slid the small ziplock bag forward on the table.

James and Caleb both smiled. Promising looks from my perspective, considering my hopeful expectation.

"Nothing that I know of, but I don't know everything," he replied. A sensible response. He pulled out his phone and began to research any interactions.

The warnings were difficult to ignore: 'risk of cardiovascular strain, risk of the MDMA masking the codeine's effects, risk of seizure, risk of dehydration.'

Generally with drugs there will be warnings of the worst case scenarios, however, combined with anecdotal reports of others doing the same thing, we could take a measured approach.

Now fully aware of the warnings, we moved on to reading experience reports.

'A relaxed and euphoric roll,' one user on Reddit titled their post. A 'roll' is the term used for a 'trip' or 'experience' with MDMA, just as being 'high' or 'stoned' was used for the effects of marijuana.

Many users taking a light dose of each didn't report any major adverse effects, and some suggested it was actually more pleasant than either drug used alone. Dosage was the important part to take note of here though. We concluded that perhaps if we only take one dose of MDMA each, about one hundred milligrams, we would be okay.

Understanding the risks, and taking the measured precautions, we decided it would be safe enough to partake.

TWO

We carefully measured out our one hundred milligrams each on a set of small digital scales, and portioned out the doses on plates. Since I had only purchased two doses from Caleb, he added from his own supply to make for three.

The moments leading up to taking a drug were always filled with excitement and anticipation, knowing that something good was to come, and each step in the ritual being more exciting than the last.

I licked my fingers, pressed them onto the brown crystals that was the MDMA, and licked my fingers again. It tasted terrible, in a way that left a definite chemical signature, and so I had a sip of the painstop drink to wash it down.

For the next hour we talked, and as we talked we drank more cough syrup, and as we drank, the MDMA was starting to take effect. We didn't really notice it at first as it crept in, until there was an "aha" moment when we realised we were pretty fucked up. That moment hit us after about an hour and a half.

My insides felt warm and cosy, and I fell in love with everything that I saw. The room was so comfortable, and it felt so nice that we all knew each other. I suddenly had compassion for and was so grateful for everything. Any feeling of tiredness was removed from my mind, and I was euphoric. And as all of these feelings were washing through us all, we continued to have more cough syrup.

It was always in times like these when my perception of the world had changed so dramatically for the better, that made me question what true reality is. How could it be that one moment I feel unsure about life, and another I feel so certain, excited and happy about everything, with both feeling equally as real as each other. This demonstrated to me early on the subjectivity of reality.

I understood from the research we had done that this cough syrup contained the antihistamine promethazine, but I was not aware that this drug had its own set of effects at high doses. We so naively overlooked this, so focussed on the drugs we knew, codeine and MDMA, and continued to consume more and more of the syrup.

The conversation in the room continued more easily and seemingly without the need to think. It was as if we flowed off of one another, each reply so obvious that we almost just fell into it. I wasn't even aware of what we were talking about anymore, and when I tried to focus, I could only remember at a maximum the last two or three things that were said.

Then silence, followed by a:

"Yeah I'll get a large coke and a cheeseburger... wait what!"

Everyone was looking at me.

"I thought I was just at McDonald's, what the fuck!" I was astonished and in shock at what I had just experienced.

Everyone laughed. For some reason it was funny at the time to see someone so fucked up that they didn't know where they were, and while I understood why they were laughing, I wondered how I could be entirely absorbed into a fictional reality, seeing it in front of me in the same way that I saw the real world.

This continued to happen to all of us - a state of confusion and laughter each time we realised we were dreaming while awake. And when I snapped out of these occurrences, I could again see the real world, however as I looked at the room closely, it appeared there was a pattern overlaying everything I saw. Circles of purple and green in a grid like fashion made up my whole vision.

I looked at the blank wall of the lounge room, as its absence of anything but white made it the best and clearest thing to be able to observe the patterns on. 'What is that? What are they?' I thought to myself.

"Close the door," I said, believing it was the most appropriate thing to say in response to whatever James had said before.

"Yeah alright but only if you get me a sour patch kid from work," James said.

"Yeah sure I remember that's what mum said," I replied.

Over an hour or so of this passed, and it was at this point I realised that I could no longer remember what the beginning of the sentence that I was saying was. My mind was guessing and believing whatever it could in order to continue speaking.

We all were the same. Our language was turning nonsensical, yet to us it felt as real and as meaningful as any normal conversation. It was an ever going generation of related content that coherently made no sense.

With no memory, it felt to us as being perfectly present whilst traveling from situation to situation. Everything always felt like it had always been as it was, whilst also feeling brand new. This was the perfect escape.

I was at McDonald's ordering food, and then fishing with my brother, and then smoking a cigarette with a friend, and it all felt real. It was like we were vividly dreaming while awake, but every so often we would truly wake up again and become lucid, and realise in amazement as to what was happening.

"I reckon he's just saying it."

"Yeah well if I had a chance to buy one I would've."

"For sure a dam would be, but what if I had been walking... wait a second what the fuck!?"

"What?"

"I thought we were at the clothes line having a cigarette."

"Wait what the fuck!"

"Yeah what the fuck is going on!?"

We were all as confused as each other, yet always seemingly on the same page and agreeing with whatever nonsense the others were saying.

And each and every time I would snap out of whatever waking dream I was in, I would smile in astonishment again. It was a lucid experience of magic, as I went from waking dream to waking dream, believing each to be as real as the one before.

THREE

I woke up from a series of confused dreams with a heavy head. The sun shined through the westward windows blinds into my eyes, illuminating the dust in the room with an orange ray. It must've been late afternoon.

I'd slept on the couch that night, and only remembered a slow merge from reality to dreams as I was in between being asleep and awake. I got up into a sitting position and looked around.

I assumed James was in his room sleeping still, guessing by the closed door, but Caleb's door was open, and he wasn't inside. Perhaps he'd headed out already.

I made my way up the hallway to the kitchen and boiled the kettle. The sound of rumbling grew louder as I scooped a teaspoon of instant coffee into a mug.

Click - the kettle was done, and I poured the water from it into my mug that quickly emanated a scent of coffee to my nose. How good this afternoon morning was already, with a cup of coffee and an already chopped up mix.

I found my way back to the lounge, and sat with a blanket around my legs. A cosy start, I thought, safe, inside, and with everything I need already here. The perfect day to stay in.

The house was still quite tidy considering the night before, and although it wasn't luxury, it was one that provided a certain comfort and homey feeling.

My coffee steamed in that orange sun beam, and as I sipped it and prepared to smoke the weed in front of me, I was reflecting on the night before.

I still couldn't believe the lucidity of the waking dreams I had experienced. I wondered how that was possible, and my curiosity forced me to do some research.

This made for the perfect combination of things to enjoy - coffee, weed, and researching drugs. Each provided their own amount of dopamine, as the reward centers in my brain were wired perfectly to enjoy them all, especially combined.

I searched, "effects of promethazine in high doses" - the page displayed: 'Disorientation, confusion, sedation.'

"What class of drug is promethazine?" - 'Anticholinergic.'

"Mechanism of action of anticholinergics?" - 'Works on the acetylcholine receptors in the brain.'

"Drugs that work on acetylcholine receptors?" - 'Diphenhydramine, doxylamine, promethazine, atropine, hyoscine.'

"Diphenhydramine" - 'Diphenhydramine, or DPH, is used in over-the-counter cough medicine... Multiple cases of abuse and addiction have been documented. Recreational users report calming effects, mild euphoria, and hallucinations as the desired effects of the drug.'

"Diphenhydramine experience" - multiple 'trip reports' showed on the screen. I read through many people reporting seeing spiders on the walls, shadow people, and sometimes at high doses, being convinced of being elsewhere in a waking dream-like state.

Yet again, I had discovered for myself another whole class of substances with its own unique set of effects, and it felt as if I was discovering another colour in the spectrum of my mind.

I continued through the list of substances.

"Hyoscine" - 'Hyoscine, also known as scopolamine, is a medication used to treat various conditions, including motion sickness, postoperative nausea and vomiting. Hyoscine has been used recreationally, but this is generally discouraged due to potential negative and dangerous effects.'

I came to learn that this hyoscine, or scopolamine as it was generally called, originated from a family of plants called nightshades. Many species in this family of plants feature these long and white drooping flowers, which I had seen before in gardens and alongside roads where I lived. The most commonly used were two main species, colloquially named angels trumpet, and devils trumpet.

I learned this has historically been used to induce hallucinations and make people more agreeable. It had reportedly been used in thefts where the victim, when under the influence, would help the thief steal from themselves.

One report explained of someone helping a thief carry their own belongings from their own house into the thief's vehicle, as if in a highly suggestible trance. There were also many reports of it being used spiritually and in shamanic traditions to help access other realms.

This was very aligned with our experience the night prior, when we were all agreeing with each other without knowing what we were talking about. Perhaps when in this state someone could tell you what dream you are in, and you would believe it entirely without hesitation.

What surprised me the most about this particular drug, scopolamine, is despite its potency and risks, it was sold over the counter at pharmacies as a medication for travel sickness. The brand most commonly available not only included the potent drug in the pill, but also caffeine to fight against any sedation the medication caused.

It was a pharmacy grade and legal equivalent to our previous nights concoction, minus the codeine. An anticholinergic for the trippy effects, and a stimulant to keep me awake long enough to enjoy them.

The find was almost too perfect. How could there be something seemingly so powerful yet readily sold without prescription, in a perfect balance for recreational effects?

My coffee was coming to an end, with only a sip left. It was a successful endeavour of research, and as the weekend grew to a close, with a night of rest ahead, I kept my new found knowledge conscious for when an opportunity arose.

FOUR

The week passed by as normal, although my life somehow had a newfound magic attached to it. I found in moments that I stared at objects closely, trying to notice what they are made from in my perception.

Things were exactly as they were before, yet felt less solid, and more imaginary. Life had a more dreamlike quality to it, as I questioned how I could really know if what I saw was real. And every so often that week, when I focussed on what I was looking at in the right way, I could see a glimpse of the green and purple circles once again.

It took me quite some weeks to contemplate and read on the matter before coming across a book that explained the world as being made of light. I had heard this before as some corner of my mind found the concept familiar, but it had never held as much meaning as right now.

It was perhaps a month after that initial experience that I received the impulse to enter a chemist as I walked past it.

I was at the shops of my local city, in a large shopping centre that spanned two sides of the main road and was connected by an indoor bridge. Right next to the grocery store that I went to was a chemist, and as I walked past it, it triggered my mind to remember the information I had learned a month earlier.

I knew that with my personality type, I should be very careful with my drug use, especially of those with major effects. I smoked weed most days, under the impression that it wasn't going to ruin my life, but I knew that heavier drugs like MDMA, and now this new class of potent drugs, had the potential to make my life spiral out of control quickly.

I thought I should at least check the chemist just to see if it was there. 'I don't have to buy any,' I thought to myself. Really, this was an excuse my mind gave itself to be able to get as close to the drug as I would allow it to in that moment.

There was a deep part of me that often gripped my conscious mind and led me down a seemingly reasonable path of agreement towards taking whatever drug I wanted to do but knew I shouldn't. It always felt like I was making the decision to get high, and that I was okay with it. It was a clever self-deception that some would call addiction, others demons.

I entered the shop and looked to my right towards all the aisles, reading the signs that advised what each aisle stocked. I walked to the one that had the travel sickness medication.

There it was on the shelf; a small white and blue package with the brand name printed on the front. A portal to another world was in front of me, my mind already preempting the feeling of the drug and anticipating what insights I might gain from it.

My hand reached forward to pick it up, and I read the information on the box.

'Hyoscine hydrobromide 200 micrograms.
Dimenhydrinate 50mg
Caffeine 20mg'.

I had to research what dose I would need to get the effects I wanted. I had found some information online that I converted into the number of pills I would need to take, and it seemed it was anywhere from five to ten to have a trip-like experience.

I knew I probably shouldn't be buying it, but then again could somehow not find any reason I shouldn't. 'You're going to do it eventually,' I told myself, 'I can just save it for when I want to do it. At least then I know I've got it'.

It seemed reasonable enough. It was the final agreeable moment my mind needed to convince me to buy the drug, and my mental justifications soon morphed into: 'If you just have it tonight, and have the weekend to recover, there isn't any reason that would be a problem'. My mind told me these things, and I agreed with them.

I took just one box containing ten tablets to the counter, and paid for it.

I now held my altered conscious experience in my hands.

FIVE

I arrived home and unpacked my things. I lived in a room in the shed out the back of my parents' house, which suited me perfectly for what I wanted in my life at that time. It was my retreat, away from the real world; a room full of art books, a place to record music, and a place to get high. It was up a set of industrial looking grated metal stairs that vibrated with a hum after every step.

I put away the food I'd bought into the fridge, and put the kettle on for a herbal tea. I had a vast collection of herbs, all from blue lotus to chamomile to mugwort, each with their own subtle effects, and each complementing different activities and times for me. This was a time to relax, and so I opted for chamomile, valerian, and passionflower, the optimal soothing combination I had at the time.

I sat on the couch in my room, where I looked ahead at the tea that steamed from its mug, illuminated by the lamp on the glass table in front of me. This, and the plant on my table, worked well with the art books and pens to create quite a comfortable scene. But there it also sat, quite contrasting to the other elements, a packet of travel sickness tablets, awaiting.

I decided with the tea it was the right moment to do some research before and during trying the new drug. Like eating popcorn at a movie, researching drug effects was the perfect accompaniment to waiting for the effects to start working. It added to the excitement and anticipation, my mind trying to imagine what it would feel like. And so I began with four tablets, cautioning at first when entering unfamiliar territory.

I sipped my tea and began reading, and while I did I tried to pay attention to how I was feeling and what I was seeing. I tried to notice those circles again in my vision, focusing my eyes to look for them. I wanted to know what those patterns were last time, and if they could consistently come back.

There were accounts online of people consuming the drug from the seeds of the datura plant. This was a much more dangerous way of consumption, as each seed was dosed differently, and the difference in dosage between hallucinating and serious trouble can be small.

Many of those accounts resulted in people leaving their homes, unknowingly following a series of hallucinations in which they travelled far distances, and only becoming conscious again once they were in the next town or city.

It was a risk I hadn't thought of, and as I pondered how to combat this if it was to occur, I began feeling a slight effect on my eyes and mouth. They felt drier than before, and when I checked my face in the mirror I noticed my pupils were dilated. Something was happening.

Comfortable with how I was feeling, I decided that having more was safe. I understood that with the tablets containing a carefully dosed amount in each I was able to know exactly how much I have had and can still have. I doubled my initial dose by swallowing another four tablets. I felt that this would probably be enough for the night to provide me with strong effects.

The dryness in my eyes and mouth continued to increase for some time. I sipped my tea to try to combat the dryness, and listened to music while I waited. After an hour or two, more and different effects started.

I noticed in my vision that small sparks of green light appeared in the corners and edges of objects I was looking at. I looked closely at the circular edge around the top of my tea cup, and I could see a dancing buzz of green electricity.

It was almost as if at the seams of where surfaces met there was an electric line that had a holographic appearance. This appeared on every sharp junction point of any surfaces, most noticeably the edges of the table and the corners of the room.

I knew those patterns I had seen before were near, and focussed on those corners to try to see more.

And as I stared, I continued my conversation with my friend:

"So maybe we can study that together the day before," I said.

"I'll come to yours if that works then straight after we can go do something for the weekend", he replied.

"Sounds good," I agreed, "... wait what?"

My friend vanished, and so did the forest around me. The trees I thought I was walking past turned back into the bricks of my room wall, and the ground back into my glass table. It had started.

SIX

I had to be aware to not fall into some waking dream that led me out of my room. I knew how important this was, as being by myself and this far intoxicated, it was a very serious risk.

I stared at the glass table in front of me, which now seemed to be covered in a greenish purple overlay of some sort of pattern, very similar to what I had seen in the past.

"What is that?" I asked myself while I still could.

I sat back in my chair and wrapped a blanket tightly around me. "Don't go anywhere, stay right here and just try to sleep," I told myself, knowing well that real sleep was unlikely.

"Stay right here..." I told myself again.

I closed my eyes, and I could see the normal blackness behind my eyelids, but in the blackness was a green holographic pattern. It was that same overlay, but with the blackness of my closed eyes it was isolated, seemingly revealing another space of reality that I couldn't see before.

As my thinking drifted, contemplating what I was seeing, I seemed to lose conscious control over the train of thought that was developing. I was slipping.

An amnesic dream state followed, and I became conscious of the fact that I was walking. It made sense to be walking, I know I had left for a reason, and that I was going somewhere I needed to go.

But I was lucky to have moments of lucidity every so often. In a moment of break from my dream state, I became conscious enough to actually ask myself, "Where am I going? I must find my way home."

And so I looked for my house along the road I was on, and saw a door that I believed might be the one I had left from. The house seemed familiar. In fact it was my house, there was no doubt.

It was a nice day out. I assumed it must have been around three o'clock, and the sun was still well in the sky. I walked to the front door and knocked.

"Hopefully someone will let me in", I said to myself as I waited.

"Who are you?!", an elderly lady answered the door, clearly alarmed at an unknown visitor, and as she spoke, the sky turned dark and the familiar house became unfamiliar.

I really did think it was day time and that this was my house, but when her alarmed voice startled me into waking from a dream state once again, and the sky turned black and the house transformed, I realised what had happened.

"I thought this was my house, I'm so sorry I don't know where I am!" I sincerely apologised to the lady, hoping she would understand. And so I left as quickly as I could, now running up the road I had come, and telling my mind to not do that again.

My heart was beating faster, and my hands began to sweat. "Please don't knock on any more doors, just find your way home." I begged myself, now almost in panic, but I understood I needed to remain calm.

I was now awakening from a dream state again, this time with no recollection of any hallucinations, only a lapse in time. And as I became aware, my hand was in front of me already knocking at what appeared to be another door.

"Ah not again!" I stopped my knocking and turned around to leave.

I was in trouble now, I could feel it. I was losing control of where I was ending up and what I was doing. I didn't know how far from home I had gone, and wasn't sure when the next dream state would take me. I felt I was in the middle of chaos.

I found myself sitting in the back yard of my friend's house, by a clothesline, smoking a cigarette and talking. It was a familiar scenario to me. And while I talked and smoked with my friend, it appeared to me that I was working to craft a table.

I had the wood in front of me, sanding it, cutting it, screwing it together. I was quite proud of my work. And when it was complete I felt a sense of ownership over what I had created. This was my table, and I made it myself. I remember all the details clearly, certain of the process I had taken to make it, vividly remembering being a part of its creation.

I was startled by the opening of the sliding door from the house to the backyard.

"Who are you?!" A woman said to me in a tone that was hostile and confronting. My cigarette vanished from my mouth, and my friend I had been chatting with abandoned me by disappearing into the air. I realised I was alone at this back table, talking with myself.

"I'm so sorry, I don't know what's going on! This keeps happening," I told her with sincerity and fear in my tone.

And as I spoke I got up, ready to leave, and when I stood I grabbed the table in front of me. 'My table', I thought, 'that I'd spent so long creating.'

"You're stealing!" The woman screamed at me.

"I'm sorry I thought it was mine!"

I dropped the table and ran for the gate that let me back onto the street. 'I can't do that again', I thought, 'that's got to be the last time.'

I focussed all of the conscious ability I had left into finding my way back home, and as I drifted into another dream state again, and awoke from it shortly after, I found it was morning, and I was back in my room.

SEVEN

A wave of relief washed over me like no other feeling of relief I had ever felt before. 'I'm safe', I thought, 'Was that all a dream?'. I was only now finally awakening from my altered state and remembering the confusion of the night before.

I was seated in the chair still, and tucked in with my blanket, as if I had never left. I noticed the table in front of me presented the packet of travel sickness medication, showcasing its empty blister pack. All ten pills were gone, and I don't remember taking the last two. Maybe all ten was too much.

Having awoken at my home was a comfort though, knowing perhaps the night could be left where it was and not follow me.

I made my way down the metal stairs to leave the shed, and walked to the kitchen of the main house. And as I looked up the hallway and out of the window next to the front door, I could see outside, there was a police car and two officers.

I had this feeling that it might have been another dream. How could I know what was real if what I had experienced the night before was not real, yet felt real to me? What if I still was in a dream, how would I know? And this led me to ask, what is it that creates what I see? What is it made from, and what am I really looking at?

But my endless pondering over what is real and what is not could not change the reality I faced. The police did appear to be real, I was pretty sure they were, and I needed to figure out my next move.

Maybe they were here for something unrelated, and it was a strange coincidence?

I walked towards the door, calmly ready to face whatever consequences I had to, my mindset already in acceptance.

"Hello?" I asked as I opened the door.

Somehow they knew my name, and that I was the individual causing the disturbances the night prior. I would guess that one of those houses had security cameras, and so they could identify me, or trace me back to here. I'll never truly know.

I was taken to the police station, still drowsy and slightly dazed and confused. They seated me in a holding cell of perspex to observe me, and once I was sober enough to be fully coherent, they asked me questions.

"I was confused after taking these drugs," I told them. "It said online they would cause hallucinations, but I shouldn't have done it by myself."

I was blatantly honest with them. Fully transparent. And so they said they appreciated this and let me go.

How fortunate I was to be let off so easily. For a brief moment I noticed the shift in my perspective between being free and not being free. I should appreciate it always, but this memory fades, and my freedom becomes an under-appreciated part of my experience.

What did not fade, however, was a faint sparkle of green light that appeared as I stared at the corners and edges of anything with corners and edges. It was similar to a visual snow, that when I looked at it more closely, it revealed itself to be a visually sharp buzzing of electricity.

'Perhaps if I could see more, it would be shapes?' I wondered.

At first it was easy to accept that visuals like this were the result of a drug's effect on the brain. Scientists often had such descriptive language to explain a process of the mind but no real understanding of why it worked. I often would read online that 'this drug acts on this particular receptor which causes this set of effects,' however how did that manifest as the experience of seeing a particular pattern?

They then tell me the drug's effects on the mind affects my perception of the outside world. From this I understood that my perception of the outside world is constructed by my mind.

EIGHT

I had always assumed that when I looked at a tree, I was seeing that tree for what it is in reality. It is over there, and separate from me.

It was two weeks after my incident with the police. I had not returned to drugs apart from marijuana to sleep at night. Apart from this though, my days had been more or less what anyone would consider normal.

I got up at a reasonable time in the mornings, spent time with family, worked, and ate well. But always there in my vision of normal things was a green electricity, and when I focussed on it, it would every so often reveal more of itself to me.

I awoke on the Monday of that week to the white ceiling, slightly dotted with specks of green visual snow.

"Why do I still have this happening?" I asked out loud. I was more curiously asking than with any real negative emotion, as I almost enjoyed the interesting atmosphere it provided to any mundane situation.

Work was more enjoyable, as while I worked I could focus on this other thing I could see, and ponder about what it was. It felt as though I was on a path of discovering something profound, and the magic that was missing from my life since childhood had now returned. I could live with a sense of wonder again.

There was however also some concern. 'Perhaps I should be cautious of this as if it progresses and can't be reversed then I could be in big trouble.' But despite any concern, I had no fear of it. I was eager for the exercise and embraced the sense of magic it gave, which to any outsider would present itself to them as a young man entering a psychosis.

Part of my lack of concern for my visual situation arose from the research I always did. Many people shared this experience, and it has been given the name HPPD, for Hallucinogen Persisting Perception Disorder. And while many people have written of their experiences, not many had anything to say about why or how it was occurring.

I was sure to never tell anyone one that wouldn't understand, and hadn't mentioned these symptoms to anyone yet. That morning however, as this effect on my vision was still persisting, I thought it may be worth checking in with Caleb.

I got myself out of bed, boiled the kettle and prepared a coffee, and as I sat, coffee steaming in the morning sun, I called Caleb's number and waited.

After much anticipation and on what must have been the last ring, he answered.

"Hey man, how's it going? What've you been up to?" He asked.

"Yeah good. Just been working, keeping it pretty tame the last while. You?" I replied.

"I've been trying to. I had a big weekend last weekend though. We had more of that painstop here."

"Did it get all confusing again like last time I was there?"

"Yeah we were mostly drowsy first but as soon as we had some lines of M we were all confused and delirious."

I was glad to hear I wasn't the only one who had gotten themselves into that state of mind again, and after hearing about Caleb's second experience I believed my hunch to be correct about the combination of anticholinergics and stimulants.

I knew that James mostly knew what he was talking about with respect to taking drugs. Caleb was knowledgeable, but James was well read. And so I asked Caleb if James was home, and when he said he was, he passed the phone over to him.

We spoke for a short time, and I told him of my incident.

"And the caffeine is in it in the perfect amount to combat the tiredness." I told him.

"You know there is a drug I have heard of that is both at the same time. I dispensed it to a customer today. It is like a stimulant anticholinergic."

"What is it?"

"Oxybutynin. It's prescription only though." I paused to embed that name into my memory. Oxybutynin.

"Is there any chance you've experienced like lingering effects? Like with your vision?" I asked James.

"A little bit of a visual snow yeah, only in the first few days after though, it's mostly gone away now."

I suppose James didn't take the travel sickness medication two weeks prior, and so maybe that's what had caused mine to stay longer than his. And I know I shouldn't have felt happy at the news that my friend had lingering effects from drugs, but it was a comfort to know that I wasn't alone.

NINE

From that period onwards, I knew I had to be quite careful with my drug use. I knew I didn't want things to get worse, but somewhere inside me there was a yearning for deeper exploration. Some deep part of me did want it to get worse, so I could see more.

That same week, James and I were by the train line near my house, walking and talking, and approaching the train station.

"I've been wondering, what is that visual snow, like when you focus on it?" I asked James.

"What do you mean? Probably just some issue with my vision and the cones and rods of the eyes or the brain... who knows," he replied, from a very scientific and physical standpoint.

"No but I mean, when you focus on the snow, and can see a small flash of something, what is that?"

"Like I said, probably just something faulty in the mind or something lingering from the drug," James replied again as if I wasn't getting it.

He bent down to pick up a half smoked cigarette someone had left on the ground. We called these bumpers, which were the leftovers of other people's already smoked cigarettes. I liked to call them double smokes, to add a level of class to our actions. It let me feel further away from the reality of what we were doing.

"Sure it's the drug's effect on our minds or eyes that causes it, but that's not what we're seeing," I said back.

He looked confused.

"Let me explain it like this. When you imagine a tree, where is that tree that you see?" I asked.

"In my mind?" James answered.

"But where is that? If I cut open your brain I'm not going to find a tree am I? Sure your neurons fire in a certain pattern that means tree, but that's not the tree itself."

"What's the point here?"

"Well the visual snow is like the tree. It's not really in the brain, it's some non-physical place," I explained, hoping he would understand.

"I get what you mean, yeah. I've just never thought about it like that before."

I smiled. I was glad someone understood, and didn't just take my ramblings as crazy talk. This is why I had to be very careful who I spoke to about this, and why James was one of the people I could trust to understand.

"Doesn't that mean that everything we see is the same like that? And hear and touch?" James was always good at taking things a step further.

"What do you mean?"

"Whether we see something or imagine it, they're both just signals inside our brains."

"Ahuh?"

"When I experience something, my brain receives signals from the senses, and my brain interprets those signals as being what I experience. It doesn't actually hear a real sound, or see a real object; it creates that experience from the signals it receives."

"So in a way everything we experience, is not physical, in that way?" I asked.

"What we imagine and what we experience is made of the same thing." James affirmed. But I wondered what it was that it was made from, and where it existed, if not physically.

It was getting difficult to fully put our fingers on what it was we were trying to get at, but it made sense to us, and it felt profound. It was as if the line between imagination and physical reality was becoming smaller, in some way that I couldn't quite fully explain at the time.

And so it was in that moment, walking by the train line, that I felt as though I was on the cusp of uncovering something about reality that would change my experience of it forever. But I never thought to contemplate whether it was something I wanted forever. Once I uncover truths like this there is no going back, but only once it is uncovered do we know whether we want to go back.

How could I go back though? Knowing that there was more to uncover and know. Knowing there are insights to be gained, how could I ignore them?

I knew that I wanted to move forward from here, and that there were a number of routes I could take.

TEN

For me, all of the routes to uncovering these deeper truths involved drugs. I understood there was the path of meditation and spiritual inquiry, but in my mind this seemed like the longer path. I understood I could spend years working towards discovering them in life, but assumed instead I could have a few six to twelve hour experiences.

I never thought to consider the consequences of the path of drugs though. None of us did back then. We were approaching drugs with the perspective that the drugs themselves weren't inherently bad, but it was how the drugs were used that determined the outcome. James was a big believer in this.

It was still early on in our experimentation with everything; first we drank alcohol, then tried marijuana, then MDMA, cough syrup, etc. We had all heard of psychedelics, like LSD, mushrooms, and DMT, but none of us had tried them yet.

So many had talked of never seeing things the same after taking LSD, and that these drugs can help individuals attain spiritual enlightenment. They drew me towards them, yet stayed elusive for quite some time, and I understood that they would come into my life at the right moment, when I was ready.

A few weeks had passed since that day by the train tracks with James. I had called a few times over those weeks, but no one answered. I'd assumed at first that perhaps he was busy or had a problem with his phone, but every time I didn't hear from a friend for too long, anxiety always found its way into my mental space to catastrophise the situation.

Maybe James didn't want to talk to me, or was avoiding me on purpose. Maybe I said something last time that I shouldn't have. Maybe he thinks I'm crazy. My anxiety was quite selfish in the sense that I always worried that it was something to do with me, and not that I should be concerned about the other person.

And so even though we spoke less often, I called Caleb. Since he lived with James, he was the next best contact to get through.

"Hey man, how're things going?" I asked.

"Yeah good man, yourself?"

"Yeah good too, can't really complain... I haven't heard from James in a while hey."

Caleb paused before he spoke. "You should come down sometime," he said, not fully addressing my mention of James.

"Yeah I think I will."

"Yeah... I—I'll fill you in when you get down," Caleb said.

I didn't interpret that as being anything good, but couldn't jump to conclusions yet. I had a feeling though that something had happened.

I put my phone down, and got to packing. I didn't need much, just a few changes of clothes, some food for the trip, a bottle of water, and made sure I brought some tobacco and a lighter. Once I was ready, I locked the door on the way out, and began walking to the train station.

The path to the station ran behind an industrial estate that was down the street from my house, and on the opposite side was a creek and an abundance of plant life behind a chain-link fence. I often thought it would be a great place to grow something one day.

The train from mine to James and Caleb's was about an hour and a half. I got on, and watched the mountains pass on one side as the ocean drifted in and out of view on the other. I suppose it wasn't the most productive time for me, but it was good down time. It was a great excuse to not do anything and not feel guilty about it, because I was travelling.

When I finally arrived at my friend's house, James wasn't there. It was just Caleb at home, who welcomed me in, and we went to the lounge room to catch up.

It'd been months since I was last there, consuming cough syrup and MDMA with both of them. But now the energy had changed, and there was a scent of concern in the room.

"I tried DMT last week," Caleb said, trying to fill the air with something interesting and bring attention away from the atmosphere. "I got some from the guy I get my other stuff off."

"What was it like?" I asked.

"It's like a powder."

"I mean the experience?" Something seemed really off. I knew something was on Caleb's mind for him to be acting like this.

"You're meant to smoke it and hold it in for as long as you can," he paused, gathering his thoughts, "they say three hits is what you're meant to have to break through," he continued, "but I decided to try to just put it all in one hit."

"After I inhaled and held, it sort of felt like I was in a dream that faded quickly after I woke up. I remember I inhaled, then there was something about a pink ice cream van on the main street, it passed me, then I sort of came to."

Such a brief and vague description, I wanted more detail.

"Did you gain anything from it?" I asked.

"Not sure. It was definitely intense. I feel like it's something you'd like. I know you're into questioning reality and stuff, I could imagine you'd love it."

Caleb was shy of being deep sometimes. I often felt I would only get to a surface level with him when discussing things, and that he had more he wanted to say but held within him.

"I definitely want to try it someday. Where's James at? Did he do it too?" I asked as I looked around the room, drawing attention to his clear absence.

I waited as he thought, and then he explained that James had missed out on doing the DMT. And since he had missed out, he wanted to make up for the experience by doing any other psychedelic.

None of us had tried psychedelics before, and so didn't know what to expect from them. We didn't understand the difference between the experience of LSD and DMT.

Caleb went on.

"... and the only other psychedelic we could get was acid. He had two tabs, which was probably way too much, especially for a first time. Anyway about two hours in he started freaking out."

I continued listening, relaxing back into the lounge and focusing on the story as it unfolded in my mind.

"James, very scientifically minded, had the brilliant idea that taking meth would pull him out of any bad thoughts or experiences. He explained 'it's just an amphetamine that will cause positive emotions and a feeling of ecstasy, and so should stop the bad trip.'"

It was the stupidest thing I had ever heard, yet also made some sense when explained in the way Caleb said it.

"I get the reasoning, but I feel like there would have been a lot of solutions I would've tried before meth," I said.

Caleb explained that James had got some meth off an old acquaintance from school, and when he took it, he blacked out. He'd been in the hospital since. This explained why I hadn't heard from him in so long.

How quickly it can all change, I thought. I need to be very careful, especially with my inward journey. I need to choose wisely which drugs I take in my journey, as if I go down the wrong path, I may not be able to come back.

I didn't hear from James for several more weeks, until he got out. In that time, I ensured I became well researched in each type of psychedelic, so I could choose which would be the best for me. After James's incident, I was a bit hesitant, and very cautious. 'As long as I don't do meth though,' I thought, 'I should be fine.'

ELEVEN

I visited James the weekend after he got out, about three weeks after I saw Caleb and found out what happened. I expected James would be normal, as he always had been. At this moment in life, I wasn't aware of how lasting some actions can be. I believed things would mostly continue as they had before.

"Hey man," I said as I walked in his front door.

"Hey bro," he replied.

He seemed normal.

We sat in the lounge room as he filled me in on what happened in the hospital, and what happened on the night it all occurred.

"... so then he offered me some meth, and I thought about it, and in that moment it made sense. It'd force me to be positive, so my trip would turn around," he told me, "but it wasn't long after I had it where I don't know really what happened... I don't remember anything until I came to, in the hospital."

I got up to go to the kitchen and grab a drink.

"Are you even listening to me?" James's tone was serious and confrontational.

"Yeah man I'm just gonna grab a drink real quick."

"This whole time you've been here you haven't been very receptive at all. It's like you're not present and aren't listening to me. I've found it really disrespectful."

'Perhaps I should have excused myself to get a drink,' I thought.

And then he left his own house, leaving me there in the lounge room to decide what to do next. It was the oddest thing, to watch him change like that. It was like an insecurity magnified, that he was afraid people didn't really listen to him, mixed with paranoia that it was true. His demeanor before leaving the house projected a coldness into the atmosphere. It didn't feel like the James I knew.

I thought for some minutes, half expecting James to come back, but at about minute four or five I got up and left the house as well. I was in a very awkward mental state after this.

I thought that perhaps it could have been that because I had the notion that he would be different, I treated him differently. Maybe I caused this by expecting it, and he was right. But I wasn't alone in my experience of his change.

The James I knew before was very unserious. He'd been the one who made jokes out loud in class at school, and was clever with his humour. He was smart, and had great potential, but everyone

I had spoken to that had seen him around this time all sensed this was a turning point for him.

As I walked down the street and away from his house, I was processing how to react. Should I feel bad? As perhaps I had wronged James. Or should I feel angry? Angry that he's just acted that way towards me for no reason. Or maybe I should feel sad that he has been changed and not take it personally.

In my slightly rattled state, my sensibility was dampened, and I walked to the shops to find something I had been meaning to try for some time. If I could find an independent local store it would be better, but if not, the larger chain grocery stores would do.

I visited a few Asian and middle eastern grocers to check. I'd been told they tended to have lesser known brands, and less heavily washed seeds, but each one I went to didn't seem to have poppy seeds in stock.

And so after not finding them in smaller stores, I proceeded to the large supermarket. Here, I bought three tubs of poppy seeds, three quarters of a kilogram worth, believing this should be enough. It was fifteen dollars all up, which I thought was quite cheap for what I was getting.

I then took myself and my seeds to catch the train home.

I had read some weeks ago that some people used poppy seeds to get high, as they are from the opium poppy. And after researching more on the train ride home, I learned that opium comes from the seed pods of the plant, and so these seeds had been soaked in opium before being harvested.

Although the seeds are usually thoroughly washed before being sold, there are some remaining opiates inside and on the seeds, and they are usually stronger when they're from smaller grocers who get their produce from different sources.

It was typical research for an addict, trying to source real, legal and cheap ways to get high. This was a holy grail of a find for someone conducting this type of research. If this worked, not only was this affordable and legal, it was also very accessible. I was realising that this was also dangerous.

My train stopped at the station a few blocks away from my house, and I walked along the path behind the industrial estate towards my street, admiring all of the plants behind the fence. I wondered which of these plants might have psychoactive effects if only humans had tested them. I wondered how many undiscovered drugs there were out in nature growing freely.

As I reached my street and turned onto it, I was running over the plan in my head. I would get home, fill a large bottle of water, pour the seeds in, and shake the bottle up for a good few minutes.

Then I would crack the lid just enough for me to pour the liquid out but keep the seeds in the bottle.

Once I got home, I did this almost immediately, and I tasted the "poppy seed tea" as it was called. It was slightly bitter, and a grey brown sort of colour. I had to be careful to not have too much, as the dosage with these seeds can vary greatly depending how much they have been washed.

As I waited, I occupied myself with some drawing, and soon, I started to feel warm and light. The intensity gradually grew over the next hours, and I felt drowsy and floaty. My eyes had a comfortable heaviness that felt very pleasant.

'This is good', I thought, as I looked back at the used bottle, still with damp seeds inside.

They were small seeds, and very hard to focus on in this state, but I tried. I focussed on the singular point in space that a particular seed occupied, and a glimmer of green and purple revealed itself to be there within it.

TWELVE

I woke the next day, still feeling somewhat comfortable and drowsy, and got up to boil the kettle. It was an overcast day, and looked like it might rain, and so when I poured my coffee, the heat and steam comforted my soul and warmed my bones.

Comfortable and drowsy yet being slowly stimulated was like breathing fresh air after smog, and regaining some clarity after fog. Opposites mostly tend to compliment each other. And so that first sip of that coffee that morning was refreshing, and perfectly satisfied something within me.

I looked again at the bottle of seeds, and it appeared inflated and hard. There was a pressure building inside. I undid the cap and there was a hissing of gas escaping the bottle, and as I looked closer at the seeds it seemed as if some were at the very beginning of germination. They had swelled and produced evidence of some growth, though at this stage it was very unclear.

I had some pots of plants outside my window that I watered every so often and watched, and so it was fairly easy for me to pour some of these seeds from the bottle into those pots.

The rest I brought with me as I walked up the street and turned onto the path that went behind the industrial estate. I looked at the plants on the other side of the chain-link fence and acknowledged that this was the perfect place for the seeds to thrive. I supposed the water in the stream that ran in the middle of it all was responsible for how lush everything looked.

I glanced up and down the path to make sure no one else was there that could see, and when I confirmed it was all clear, I emptied the bottle by flicking it around so that all the seeds could escape the end. They flew towards the other side of the fence, landing among all the other plants. Some landed in better positions than others, and many landed in places I could have confidence in.

I put the bottle back in my bag and left towards the train station.

With another hour and a half train ride ahead to the town my friends lived in, I was in a peaceful state and ready to relax. I looked forward to viewing the beautiful coastal scenery of beaches and bushland and cliffs. I enjoyed that time to myself, watching the natural world pass by while organising my thoughts.

I arrived at the station with five minutes to spare before the train arrived, and so I walked to the end of the platform to smoke a cigarette. I was completely unaware of what was to come that day, fully present, and enjoying the moment for what it was.

Half of a cigarette was all I needed, and so I threw it with about half left onto the ground and stepped on it to put it out - a frivolous move - usually I would have saved it. There was a cafe inside the train station, and I could feel in the air that rain may be on its way. 'How perfect a coffee would be,' I thought, so I walked quickly to ensure I had time to order.

When the train arrived, I took my coffee from the man working the cafe and entered the doors of the train carriage to find a seat. The carriage was relatively empty and dully lit by the dampened sun outside. Rain was starting to leave long wet marks along the window, and when I leaned against it after I sat down it felt cold on my cheek.

It was a cosy trip ahead. The coffee warmed my hands, and everything in that moment was bliss.

And just as I was relaxing into a deep sense of contentment, I heard someone call out my name from behind me.

I quickly turned my head. It was James.

"Are you following me?" He asked.

I got up to approach him. "Nah man, just heading down the coast," I said.

He grabbed me by the shirt and pushed me up against the wall. I was shaking, and I could feel the adrenaline rush through me. I pushed him off.

I was always very confrontation averse, and so this was unfamiliar and uncomfortable territory for me. Do I bash him? Do I keep hitting, aiming for the head mostly? That wasn't in my nature, but what I always imagined was expected in a scenario like this.

I told him I wasn't following him, and that I was actually headed down to his place for the weekend. It's so interesting that James was unaware, as I had only organised this with Caleb. We had become so distant recently that Caleb was the only person I could talk to about me coming over.

Sometimes, however, I do wonder if the universe causes certain events to happen for a reason. It is as if, after our last meeting the day before, we were meant to run into each other again — to make things right before I turned up at his house without him knowing.

We talked that train ride, and by the time we arrived at our station, we were laughing. It was as if nothing had ever happened.

We started to walk from the station to his house. It was about a forty-five-minute journey, going along the highway that would become the main street of town. We didn't mind walking, as we were used to it, and as we reached the point where the highway became the main street, I looked ahead of me towards all of the shops. Further up ahead, driving on the road, was a pink ice cream truck.

THIRTEEN

The ice cream truck drove towards us, and suddenly Caleb's name came to mind. Then, as it passed me and James, I noticed on the other side of the road was Caleb walking in our direction.

"Caleb!" I called out, while making sure the street was clear, and running across the road.

"Woah! I just had Deja Vu," Caleb said to me. And right then, when Caleb said that, a car smashed into my side.

I was rolling and bouncing across the road until I found my place to rest some way away from where I was hit. I laid on my back, feeling defeated, but alive, and looked up at the sky above. The clouds causing the earlier rain were beginning to part, revealing a blue that brought me peace.

But as pleasant as the sky was, it was contrasted by the pain that began to rise in all parts of my body. My right leg felt numb from the intensity, like a heat so hot it turns cold. And so I stayed still, hoping the driver or someone would come to my aid. 'At least I am alive,' I thought.

Before long, a lady was at my side, with a familiar and comforting voice. "We'll make sure you're alright. Stay completely still, and try not to move, in case anything has happened to your neck." And as she moved her head over mine to where I could see her face, my eyes widened, and she said my name.

It was Ashon's mum. I didn't know her extremely well, but she was a familiar face, and a nurse. Of all people, to have her there felt like an angel being sent down. My mind was trying to make sense of it all — the sequence of coincidences that day seemed implausible.

I hadn't seen my leg yet, and was advised not to look at it. It wasn't long before an ambulance arrived.

"We're here to help you mate, alright? We've got something here that'll help with the pain. Have you ever had ketamine before?"

I smiled briefly, then said no. In truth, ketamine was something I had always wanted to try, and had heard a lot about, but the opportunity never arose. It seems you have to know the right people and be in the right circles to have access to certain things.

Before receiving the relief, my mind was already unworried about all that was sore and my current condition. All I could think about was how exciting it was to be given medical grade ketamine for my first time.

"You're going to feel a small prick," the paramedic told me. I looked down at my arm and watched them insert a needle.

I quickly felt a wave wash over me, as if I was floating, and then stretching, and shrinking. The gap between my conscious mind and my body was becoming greater and greater, faster and faster. The world distorted in a way that I could not have anticipated, and I was separated from my physical self completely.

I could see the clouds above had reformed together, producing a soft rain that fell slowly, and the reflections of red and blue lights illuminated the road.

'Am I dead?' I thought. I had a feeling something serious had happened, and that my physical body was in trouble, but I had no recollection of anything. Confused and scared, I had become an unthinking observer of something I knew I was personally involved in.

FOURTEEN

My awareness lapsed, and I awoke inside a bed. I could hear the sounds of beeping and people talking around me, and there was a sterile smell in the air. I opened my eyes to see that I was in a hospital.

I was curious about the ice cream truck, and the strange sequence of events that felt like a fever dream. But it was all real, as far as I could tell.

I faced major operations and a long recovery time, but in my mind I was at peace. This was my free ticket, I thought. I would be allowed to sit around and be fed painkillers by nurses all day.

And as my time there in hospital went on, I became accustomed to the routine of the pills that gave me the effects I wanted when I wanted them.

One particular morning, about two weeks after the accident, I awoke in my bed. I was still quite drowsy and comfortable from the oxycodone and morphine they had me on, and was looking forward to my morning coffee. The combination of the simulating coffee with the comfortable drowsiness of the painkillers was a timeless pair. Opposites do complement.

I looked in front of me; my tray table was folded out ready to place my coffee on. And when the lady came, she placed it into the round indent in the plastic that was made for cups to sit in. The coffee steamed in the artificial light.

I looked at my pre-made cereal and toast, and imagined the microwave meal I would receive on plastic plates later on. And while all of this sounds plain and stale, what made it tolerable for me was the drugs I was allowed to have. In fact, I didn't just tolerate it, but enjoyed every bit of it.

The recovery took several months. My leg grew thin from not using it, and my mind grew weak from relying more and more on the medication. But soon they would run out, and I would need to search for alternatives.

It was three months after my accident, and my first week of walking on my own again. It was a Thursday, and I awoke at home and got up to get myself ready. As I drank my morning coffee, I packed an empty plastic bag into my backpack, and after I had my last sip, I left the house.

I was excited because I knew that something may wait for me at the end of my street. I walked to the cul-de-sac down the road and turned onto the path that went behind the industrial estate.

It was as if I had foreseen my need for opiates ahead of time, and by some luck prepared a crop of opium poppies ready for harvest at the perfect moment. It's strange how things work out. Those seeds that I seemingly so recently poured out through the chain-link fence had taken beautifully.

Behind the fence among the other plants was a long row of beautiful white flowers, next to stalks that hosted closed flower buds at the end. It was these buds I was after, as they contained the white milky sap called opium.

The fence was tall, which was good because it protected the flowers, but now I had to scale the fence or find a way through to reap my reward.

Up the path some ways there was a bridge that crossed the stream as it turned under the footwalk, and where this bridge's hand railing started, the chain-link fence ended. I knew that this was my entry point, where I could climb around to the other side.

The fence here had a thick layer of alive and growing vine on it that provided privacy for the short section close to the bridge.

I carefully climbed the handrailing, and stepped off to be behind the fence. Here I could walk along the fence on the side of the plants up to where the poppies grew.

I knew it was important to be quick. If someone were to walk up the path now and ask what I was doing, I had no clue what I could say. I thought that it would especially be an issue if it was someone that I knew.

So I started grabbing at all the closed buds that I could see. I wanted to get as many as I could, and the bag was filling up quickly. I would say there were perhaps a hundred or more to be picked, densely growing in a patch that spanned a maximum of ten meters.

And when I felt I had plenty, I stopped to listen for any signs of other people. When I looked up along the path I could see someone approaching. They still had some distance to travel before they came to me, but it was time to get out of there.

With my bag mostly full, I walked back up along the fence towards the bridge again. It was when I reached the bridge that I knew I had two options. With the person approaching, I could climb back onto the bridge, but if I knew the person on the path they may ask what I was doing.

My other option was to utilize this portion of fence that had the vine growing all over it. I could wait behind it, unseen, until they passed, so there was no possibility of getting caught.

My heart began to beat faster, and the speed of my thoughts followed it. I decided to play it safe and wait there, crouching behind the vines. Footsteps grew louder as I listened to the person approach. I held my breath and remained still, trying to be as quiet as possible.

When the footsteps finally reached the spot directly on the other side of the fence from where I hid, they stopped. I tried to peer through any gaps I could find in the fence to see who it was, but couldn't make out much. And then the steps continued, until I heard the person begin climbing the railing of the bridge.

I made a sound as they were about to see me, and as I did they also gasped.

"Scared me mate," I said, "what're you doing?"

"I could ask you the same," the stranger said to me.

It was a young guy, about the same age as me, with dirty blonde dread locks and a plastic bag hanging out of his pocket.

"I'd guess that most of the ripe poppies are in your bag?" He said, clearly noticing that in my backpack was a plastic bag lining the inside.

"I'm sure you'll find some up there still, I sort of rushed cause I could see you coming," I told him, "and if you can replant what you take, maybe we can keep this alive up here."

"I'll keep the seeds I get and try to put them back here when I can," he said, then he turned and made his way along the fence towards the patch.

I left towards my home again, back along the path behind the estate, and turned onto my street. I had more than thirty poppy seed pods, and in my mind was deciding how I would prepare them.

A tea, just as I'd had before, was the most common method, and because to me it was proven I decided to stick with it.

I walked up the driveway, unlocked the door to the shed out the back, and made my way up the metal stairs that hummed with each of my steps.

As I entered my room, I placed my bag on the floor in between my lounge and the glass table in front of it. I grabbed two large empty two litre plastic bottles from the shelf near the door and filled them with warm water, and then sat on my lounge and took the plastic bag with the poppies out of my backpack.

With scissors I began to chop at the seed pods, breaking them down into smaller portions that I could fit into the ends of the bottles. When I had a fine enough collection of the shredded pods, I placed them into the ends of the bottles and shook for as long as I could bear.

When the liquid inside turned a cloudy brown colour, I knew it was close to ready. My anticipation for this experience grew through the process and I so much wanted to combine it with all the things I enjoyed to maximise the dopamine I got.

I lit some incense, and ensured the table in front of me presented well. I wiped the glass, and positioned the plants and everything so it was pleasing on the eyes.

I cracked open the lid of one bottle ever so slightly so that the liquid could pour out while the seeds remained trapped inside. I strained the liquid this way and poured it into a glass teacup.

The water was just warm enough to steam ever so slightly, mixing with the smoke of the incense as it rose from the table towards the light of the lamp.

Everything was in order. I played some ambient music in the background, something to add an atmosphere but allow me to think and fully notice how I was feeling. I reached forward, collected the glass teacup from the table, and sipped.

It was bitter, with an earthy flavour. I could see impurities through the transparent cup swirl within the tea. They must've been what I was tasting.

As I sipped I prepared some weed to smoke alongside it. I took three small nuggets of marijuana, placed them into a bowl, and began chopping them with scissors. I was beginning to feel somewhat drowsy, and first noticed a heaviness in my hands as I chopped the herb finely. The ritual of it all was something I very much enjoyed.

It wasn't long, perhaps thirty minutes, when I noticed the effects were coming on strong. I wasn't sure of the strength of the tea I had made, as I had, without much knowledge, just mixed any number of seed pods into the bottles. I hoped that I hadn't taken too much. And as it so often was, no one was there to watch me to make sure that I would be okay.

The marijuana I was chopping now had a uniform consistency; it was perfectly even all the way through. And so I packed it into a pipe, and lit it with a lighter while inhaling. The smoke was soothing to my soul, and the comforting wave of a warm blanket that the weed provided washed over my mind and body.

The relaxing effects of the weed were even more pronounced with the poppy seed tea in my system, and they synergised to take me to a place void of troubles. I felt in perfect comfort and bliss. It was the correct level of drowsy and awake to fall into an in between place where everything and nothing existed at once. Some call it nodding — not fully asleep, not fully awake.

From what I could think of at that moment, my life had no real problems. Any stressor or out of order thing seemingly hid behind the chemical protection of the tea and weed. I couldn't see what was wrong, and so it didn't exist. How alluring this feeling would become.

I still had most of the tea left. Of the two bottles I had made, there was probably about three litres that remained. I knew that with the way I was feeling I didn't need any more, and so I put it in the fridge to store for another time.

I was amazed at how efficient this had been. For virtually no money, I could have many doses of this tea. I tried to further distill this thought by thinking of how I could make this even more efficient.

I understood that there were certain drugs that could make the effects of the tea even stronger. Promethazine was one of them. I remembered it was what was in that cough syrup I took with Caleb and James, all the way back at the beginning of this journey.

And so as I laid in bed, I took a mental note of this, and rested my head on my pillow. Very quickly, I was in a deep sleep.

FIFTEEN

I awoke with drowsiness and a heavy head. The sun was shining through the windows at a steep angle, suggesting it was high in the sky already. The room was warm and I was sweaty. I needed to crack a window.

As I did, a cold breeze blew in, which gave a chill to my wet skin. I wasn't sure what I had on for the day yet. I knew a shower was a good first step, and so I grabbed my towel and walked down the stairs towards the bathroom.

As I showered, I let my mind organize itself. I wondered what James and Caleb had been up to, and thought about all the experiences I'd had recently had, and which ones I would like to do again.

I turned the shower off, dried myself, and headed back up to my room, where I looked for my phone. It was a Friday, and I thought that perhaps James and Caleb would be free and keen on hanging out. This would be our first time properly catching up since I had fully recovered.

I still had three litres of tea left, and so when I called Caleb and he told me to come to his house for the weekend, I packed the tea into my bag and left for the train station.

It had been so long now since I had questioned my reality at all. I was perfectly placed back into the midst of an unquestioned existence, where I accepted things as they were because that is how I expected them to be. All traces of the visual snow and green and purple circles had disappeared, and had almost been forgotten about.

When I arrived at Caleb's, I opened my bag to reveal the poppy seed tea.

"It looks disgusting," Caleb said. He wasn't wrong, it didn't look appealing at all, and now that it had sat for a day it looked even less pleasant. Soggy bits of flower pods floated in murky water. But it didn't matter how it looked, or how it tasted. What mattered was how it felt.

"Yeah but it smashed me last night, only half a bottle," I told Caleb.

It wasn't long until more people began turning up. The air filled with chatter and laughter, and the rooms of the house became full of faces we all knew. We could feel it in the air that this night was building into something great. It would become one of those nights we all would remember but forget the specifics about.

I was seated on a recliner in the lounge room, when I got up and walked to the fridge in the kitchen to retrieve the bottles I put in there earlier.

"What is that?" Sarah asked. I didn't know her well, but we had gone to the same school, and so I mostly only knew of her.

"It's poppy seed tea. Like codeine sort of, feels really nice," I told her, "do you want a glass?"

"I'll give you a line," she offered, showing me a bag of MDMA crystals. It'd been months since I had taken MDMA.

As I poured her a glass, she crushed and lined up some of the crystal, and we sat on the floor of the kitchen and talked.

"Cheers," she said, as she raised her glass to tap it against mine.

We sipped the bitter tea, taking in the earthy taste. After that we took a rolled up note and carefully inhaled the lines of ecstasy through our nose. She went first, and then I followed.

"It burns so much," she said, eyes red and watering. It didn't take long before we started feeling more awake, more alert, yet also calm and present. We were relaxed, but focussed. It felt like total bliss.

"It's so nice we get to experience things like this," Sarah said to me.

"Yeah, it's so lucky we were born when we were, and in this area, and in this country," I replied. The drugs overwhelmed us with gratitude for our lives.

"I think about that a lot, you know", Sarah said, "how by some chance we were born here and are living now. Out of all the time that has passed, our lives aren't over and are happening right now. Unlike most of everyone who has ever lived."

"It is suspiciously strange..." I pondered on it for some moments, before asking her "Do you think about dying much?"

"Too much," she said.

Of what I knew about Sarah, one thing was that she was the party girl. Positive vibes, always dancing and smiling, and almost always on some sort of party drug.

"What people don't know," Sarah explained, "is that there's a reason I do MDMA most weekends."

"And what's that?"

"I just want to escape my own head, you know? And keep the good vibes coming," Sarah said, not realising how it might sound.

"Some might call that chasing the dragon," I told her, "but yeah I get it. It's hard to escape our thoughts, especially if they aren't great. But the drugs every weekend probably isn't helping."

Someone had to tell her. She understood, but I'm not sure if she cared.

She had a rough upbringing, like a lot of the people I knew. The school we had gone to was in the rougher part of town, so we saw a lot of poverty, and a lot of our friends came from families that were struggling. This was a shame, as so many kids with so much potential followed paths they didn't have to.

"Do you reckon Caleb would have more MDMA?" Sarah asked. Her eyes were rolling into the back of her head, and her jaw was clenching and chewing. This was common with the drug.

"Not sure, you could ask. Are you sure you need more?"

"Can't hurt." At this point she had already had four hundred milligrams. That's roughly four to five doses.

"But it can," I told her, urging her to be careful. I told her that she should at least wait a while before having too much more.

I looked at her face to really gauge where she was at, and could tell she was really beyond wasted. She was mumbling, her hands and arms in constant motion and tension, and her eyes half closed. My concern was growing. "I really don't think you should have more right now," I told her, "I'll let Caleb know not to sell it to you. I don't think he would anyway."

"You can't do that. You can't tell me what I can and can't do, and make my decisions for me. I hardly even know you," her tone was defiant and irritated. Maybe I'd crossed a line, but I was just looking out for her.

"I'm just doing it because I want you to be safe."

She got up and left the kitchen, and went to Caleb anyway, and to my surprise he did sell her more. She bought one gram, which was ten doses. Who was I to get in the way? And when all was done and Sarah offered me some, who was I to say no?

Our small conflict was immediately forgotten about in the presence of more ecstacy. We again sat on the floor in the kitchen and chatted, snorting lines every so often to keep the high afloat.

It felt like it went so quickly, but soon the music in the living room stopped, and the chatter was absent. People had left, and people were asleep. The party was over, and I had spent all of it here talking with Sarah. I really felt a strong connection with her, not in a romantic way, but I feel I really understood and got to know deep parts of her that she rarely shed light on. And as much as I wanted to continue, I decided now it was time for me to go to bed also.

We got up to move to the lounge room, which now had space after most of the people had gone. There, I smoked some weed with her as she begged me to stay awake and "keep the party going." It was seven in the morning on Saturday and the sun was in the sky already. It wasn't unlike me to stay up but I really did just want to rest.

I wished her a goodnight, and laid on the floor in James's room where there was a spot set out for me to rest. A blanket and pillow and the carpeted floor. It was comfortable enough.

Sarah left to go home, and I stared at the ceiling and waited. It was a white canvas that I could focus on, trying to see what was in the nothingness. And as the void became the focus of my attention, I could see right at the center of my vision was something.

It looked like a small circle containing a void of black, occupied by some sort of green light. And when I looked for longer it came into focus more. It appeared like a hologram made of light, displaying some mathematical geometric pattern that appeared to rotate around and in on itself. So beautiful, and so intelligent, it was very similar to what I had seen before, only more detailed.

As I continued to focus on the pattern, I lost my consciousness, and fell into a confusion of fever dreams.

I was floating as an observer. I could see a girl walking towards a house, and knocking on the door. She was let inside, and some minutes passed before she returned outside again.

My dream merged into another, where I could hear the words of a girl whimpering in a lonely search, "keep the good vibes going." Her voice shuttered, and her cold hands fell limp as she herself became an observer of her own body, hearing her own fading inner voice repeat, "keep the good vibes going." Her words slowly became quieter and more distant as she became separated from herself.

It felt as though I could see her soul leave her body. I could feel what she felt. But I tell myself this was just a dream.

SIXTEEN

When I awoke in the afternoon, the sky was orange, and I was dehydrated and sore. My jaw hurt from clenching it the night before and my head throbbed. I could feel a pain from my neck to my head when I moved, and so I moved slowly.

The room was dim, but I could see the hallway glowed an orange from the sunset, and so I slowly got myself to my feet and went to the kitchen. I made sure to have some water before making coffee.

The kettle rumbled, and it was the only sound in the house. There was no one home. I wondered where they had all gone.

I poured my cup and savoured that coffee smell once again, and walked back down the hall to the lounge room. 'I guess it's another one of these days,' I thought to myself as I placed my cup on the table.

I did want more out of my life. One of these mornings is a blessing, but too many is hell. Every so often to wake up hazy in a dusty room with the simple pleasures of weed and caffeine was nice. It was cozy. But not every morning.

But I was becoming all too used to it that its charm of being novel was fading. It was becoming sad. What hid this for me was that I usually wasn't alone. My friends and I all did it together. But today when the house was hollow and devoid of the usual characters, I especially noticed its sadness.

I found a bowl on the table next to the lounge, and in it was some weed leftover from someone, perhaps me. And so I smoked and sipped my coffee, and listened to acoustic songs as I watched the steam and smoke swirl with the dust in the red light.

I waited, and waited. The setting sun had set, and I sat in the same place for hours, smoking and drinking coffee. I knew that something felt off, but I didn't know what.

Although I drank several cups of coffee, at about ten at night I drifted into a deep and empty sleep. No dreams. It felt like a lapse in time for me from ten until I was rustled awake by James some hours later, him shaking my shoulder.

"Hey man, time to get up, we've gotta get out of here," he said to me in a tone that caused concern.

"Far out man let's just chill for a bit," I told him, lightly pushing him off of me. I was frustrated, and feeling irritated. I just wanted to sleep.

"The police are here," he said.

"What for?" I asked, my face and tone changing from irritated to concerned.

"Ahh just kidding," he smiled and pointed at my face, as if he got me.

"You actually got me," I chuckled, just agreeing to avoid unnecessary conflict and trying to see the humor in it. Maybe I would've found it funny if I wasn't so mentally depleted. "You make me a coffee and I'll get up."

James was on it. It was two in the morning. I'd only slept four hours at a maximum, and I was incredibly fatigued. James returned with a coffee.

And as I sipped, I stared at the wall, and James began talking.

"Yeah sorry I've been gone all day, got caught up helping my mum with a few things...", he continued, but his voice faded out of my awareness as all I could focus on was the faint glowing of green on the wall.

I looked harder, and could see it shimmer lightly with hints of purple wisping into view every so often. I placed all of my attention on it, and immediately it became sharp. It was a pattern made of green and purple circles that began to overlay everything. It was as if everything was made of these circles, in a hologram type of way.

"... are you there man? You all good?" To him, I was just staring blankly at a wall. He didn't see what I was seeing. And it all disappeared as soon as my attention was broken.

"You should've got angry at me saying I'm not listening and shit," I told him. There was a pause, and I waited on it almost too long, before saying "just joking" with a wide smile.

"Yeah funny," he smiled a little, "let's just go."

I finished my coffee and got up, and as we walked out of the door and up the road, we talked.

"I didn't mean to be rude before, and sorry for not listening, I've just been having this thing going on," I said. I remembered the conversation I had with James about the visual snow, and so thought he would understand.

I continued, "you ever notice how a computer has the hardware, the software and the screen?" I asked him. James nodded, letting me get the entire thought out. "It's almost like what we see in front of us is our screen. You know. It's not reality itself, but like our display of it."

"And then our mind is the software and the brain is the hardware?" James got it immediately.

"Exactly. That's it. And that's how it really is. Not just in some idea sort of way, but in reality. Everything you see is inside your mind," I told him with confidence.

"If you think like that though you'll end up crazy," James warned me. He was stern with this, I could tell.

"It doesn't mean it's wrong though."

"Yeah it doesn't man but this is the reason our brains are the way they are. We're not meant to see things like that," he said. I sort of agreed. Maybe we're not supposed to see things as they are. We're just meant to see enough to survive and reproduce.

We made our way across the park that was down the street, which headed towards town. We then crossed the road at the end of the park, and as we reached the other side I was reminded of how fun it was to wander town at night while it was empty.

The streets were bare, and we could do what we wanted. We started running, feeling the night air on our skin. We made our way onto the main street, and ran all the way along it to the other side of town. All the way past everything there was a bridge.

And when we made it to the bridge, we went down the path to the left of it that led to its under section. There was Caleb, sitting against the support beam.

"Mate you wouldn't believe what I've got for you," Caleb said to me as he reached his hand out to slap mine in greeting.

"What's that?" I asked.

He passed me an envelope.

"Open it when you get home," he told me, as we started walking out from under the other side of bridge, and up on top of it, to cross over to the other side of the river.

We walked for some time, and while we did Caleb pulled out a joint to smoke. He lit his lighter and held the flame to the end of the joint, and I could see it catch as he inhaled.

The temperature outside was cold but bearable. I was wearing a jacket and so I was comfortable. Still no one else was in sight. It was early Sunday morning, maybe three o'clock.

We passed a petrol station along the way, and stopped in to get a coffee. The shop was glowing compared to the street around it. As we walked in I could hear the buzzing of the lights, as it was so silent that the quiet sounds we tend not to notice were amplified.

The coffee machine was an automatic one, so I took a cup, placed it underneath the nozzle of the machine, and clicked 'cappuccino'.

We made our way towards the counter to pay, all three of us with a coffee each. I still felt as though there was a plan in mind that I was unaware of. It's as if I was being led somewhere by Caleb and James.

As we continued further away from town, we had now found our way towards the train station. This is where we got on a three o'clock train from this town to my home town.

The usual scenery I watched as I travelled was absent as the sky was dark and the moon was slim. And when on board I could feel a heaviness in the air as Caleb and James looked at each other, and then at me.

"We're getting out of here because Sarah... passed away man. Last night after she went home," James came out with it.

A moment of silence let those words sink in. My heart sank, and my throat closed up. I couldn't truly understand what was said in that moment... not fully.

"And I gave her the drugs that she overdosed on," Caleb said.

There was an even longer pause as I stared at them, my mind really trying to process what was said. I thought to myself that she must have gone home and taken more, and it was too much. I didn't quite know how to wrap my head around it.

"Let's not talk about this here, maybe when we get to mine or something," I said, and everyone nodded.

We made it to the station closest to mine after a long and deeply saddening journey, and when we arrived and got off, we walked from the station up a set of stairs that led to the road. The road was an overpass, and we followed it down towards the path behind the industrial estate.

It was now well past four in the morning, and the faintest gradient of light began to illuminate the horizon. I noticed the vines hanging on the fence along the pathway. The air smelled fresh, and I could see dew on the grass and leaves behind the chain-link fence.

We reached the bridge, and as we passed it and walked a little further I looked through the fence to see many bare stalks, absent of their flowers and seed pods. They had all been harvested, which was almost a relief for me. I knew if some were there I wouldn't have been able to resist.

We continued past without saying a word. I didn't mention the poppies, as it didn't feel relevant. Further along this path, past my street, and right at the very end, is a large area of bush.

The path was mostly the same the whole way along. Some more small bridges, the fence to the right, and some vegetation behind it. To the left was the estate, mostly large sheds and warehouses.

We continued until we came to the bush, and then continued into the bush, and through the bush. It took us many hours but finally we came out to a small town that was north of my own.

Here the sun was truly rising with an impressive intensity, which also somehow felt subtle due to the cool temperature of the morning. We made our way to a cafe, where we sat to eat.

"What's the plan from here then?" I asked while we ate.

"I'm just going to keep going north. I might head back when things settle, but I think it's a good time for me to travel," Caleb said.

"Won't they come looking for you?" James asked.

"Who?" Caleb replied.

"Police or whoever?" James clarified.

"Maybe, I'm not really sure of the situation exactly."

We all finished eating.

"I guess this is it then," I said.

We all said our farewells, and parted ways. Caleb left towards the train station to catch the train that headed further north. I wondered where he would end up.

James and I started walking back towards the bush we came, passing many small terrace shops along the way. And when we reached the edge of the town where the bush began, we peered inside.

"What are our plans?" I asked James.

"I'm thinking I should head home," he said.

"I'll probably do the same then," I told him.

We walked together for some time, through the bush, coming out to the path that led to my street and back to the train station. When we reached my street, I bid farewell, and he continued on towards the station.

When I got home, I walked up the stairs, into my room, and cried. For hours I cried, and fell deep into an existential depression.

What is death?

SEVENTEEN

I cried until I slept. And although I was alone and would have liked someone to lean on, sometimes these things can only be processed by yourself. Or maybe they can't fully be processed at all.

I awoke with crusted eyes and a blocked nose. My pillow was wet, and for a moment I had forgotten what had happened, but then it all came back.

I checked the time; it said it was five in the morning. The sun was barely making the east of the sky glow, and the air was cool outside.

I got to my feet, and moved to my lounge. Here, I took a cigarette paper and placed some marijuana inside. I licked the edge of the paper and rolled it up, then moved over towards the window of my room.

My room being upstairs in the back shed meant that my window led directly out to the roof of part of the first story. It was a corrugated iron roof that I had some potted plants on, in which no poppies ever sprouted. And if I stood on only where the screw line was I could exit via this window and stand out on the roof.

I peered out of the unopened window at the plants and the roof, and then into the sky where I could see the last flickers of stars before the sun's light washed them out of view.

When I slid open the window I could feel the full force of the cold morning. I didn't care about my comfort though. All I wanted to do was to forget about the weekend for a while. And so I climbed up onto the window sill, and carefully stepped over the plants, onto the screw lining.

I sat down, with my knees in my hands, and lit the joint I had rolled. That first inhale was like a warm blanket covering my mind. I smoked, and gazed at the sky as it began to glow more and more. The darkness was leaving, and the light was on its way. How I hoped this would also be true for my feelings.

When I finished smoking, I made my way back inside, and leapt down from the window sill onto the floor of my room. I walked over to my kettle and flicked it on, and as the rumbling grew louder, I noticed I was feeling somewhat better.

At the very moment that the kettle clicked and turned off, my phone began to ring, filling the void in the air that the silence of the kettle would have created. It was Ashon.

This was unusual, as I didn't really talk to him at all. My last reminder of his existence was when his mum had helped me after my accident, and my only real last memory of him was when I told him what drugs I was doing for the weekend, which gave me anxiety thinking back to it.

"Hey man," I said after I picked up.

"Hey man..." there was a clear sombreness in his tone, and a pause, "... I'm guessing you heard the news?"

"Yeah," I replied, "I still can't get my head around it."

"Same..." there was another pause, "if there's anything I can do, let me know."

"Thanks," I said.

Then there was silence, as if we didn't have much to say, but knowing we had company on the phone was comforting enough.

"I wonder what she's experiencing now... you know?" It took me by surprise, this coming from him.

"What do you mean?" I wanted him to explain.

"Like I wonder what happens after."

"Yeah, I do wonder that as well..."

I did wonder, but I never really talked about it. It felt safer to keep those thoughts in my mind, where they felt less real.

"Do you think about it much?" I asked him.

"I try not to. It scares me. I just try to focus on making money..." This wasn't the first person to say this in my life.

There was silence again.

"Can I ask you something?" He finally spoke.

"Yeah sure."

"Do you know how I could get some MDMA? Caleb's not answering his phone."

"Not sure sorry bro. I think Caleb will be away for a while."

I knew there was some reason he called other than to see how I am. But that's okay. How off putting it was though to discuss the death of a friend to MDMA, and then ask for some.

We hung up the phone, and I was left with a reminder of death, mortality, and drugs. Right when I was feeling a little bit better, the universe reminded me of how I should feel again.

I looked down at my coffee, barely steaming anymore, and took my first sip. Warm, but not hot, it was still pleasant. I sat and thought for some time, with no music, no distractions, just me and my coffee.

And after some time, I had thought about the weekend before, and where Caleb may have ended up. But soon that passed. And then I thought about how I could get high, and escape my thoughts altogether for a while. But soon that passed as well.

I was working through thoughts I usually had always run from. I thought about my family, my future, and where I am in life at this moment. I thought that one day I too shall pass, and how limited time I have.

And when I had finally thought about all I could think about, I noticed my mind was empty, and I was closer to being just an observer than I had ever been before. But in the absence of thoughts my mind would try fill the emptiness with more thoughts. I was a thinker, and had always been, and so my mind always tried to be busy.

But when I noticed any new thought arise, I would notice it as just a thought. I could see it in my mind, and identify it rather than identify with it. I realised the thought was not me, and it was in a way its own entity that I was experiencing.

And so when a thought arose, I would label it as a thought, and let it leave my mind. I could watch it float away and out of my mental space until there was an absence of thoughts again.

And in that absence, another thought arose. 'Perhaps I should go for a walk?' I thought. But instead of identifying with it, and starting to get ready for a walk, I simply noticed it was just a thought, and labelled it as such, so I could release my grip of it and allow it to float out of my mind as well.

'How freeing,' I thought, 'I can be in the present moment more fully by doing this,' and just as I thought this, I labelled it as a thought, and let it float out of my mind.

But I noticed my intention of letting thoughts float away was also a thought. And in some meta way, and without thoughts to describe what I was doing, I also saw it as a thought, and watched it also float away.

I was free from even the thought of thinking. I could no longer just think about letting my thoughts go, but had to be only a present observer, and let the thoughts leave without any internal description, label, or attachment to anything.

And as I entered this state of thoughtless awareness, and observed the world around me without any lense or story of it, I noticed a green electricity appear in the corners of my vision. It appeared in the edges of everything I observed in my room, until it grew and connected to become an overlay of green and purple circles. It encompassed my whole vision, but did not get in the way of it.

And as soon as I noticed this, I was filled with excitement, and it was that excitement that made it all go away. As quickly as the pattern appeared, it disappeared, as the many thoughts that came into my head ended the emptiness of my mind. 'What is this? Have I figured it out?' I thought.

EIGHTEEN

"Did the universe or consciousness come first?"

"What seems most obvious is that the universe was first, but I like to think it was consciousness first, although I cannot know," I replied.

"I think the idea of something exists before the thing itself. How can a tree exist without the idea of a tree existing before it?" James asked me, thinking in a way I hadn't thought before. "And so ideas, being non-physical, and being labels attributed to the world by consciousness, must exist before the physical things." James said this so confidently, as if he knew.

"What do you mean 'the labels attributed by consciousness?'"

"Well," he explained, "a chair is only a chair because we label it as such. Otherwise it is just an amalgamation of shapes. Just shapes of wood colour in some configuration. And even these shapes we can only perceive because we label them as shapes of a certain colour."

It sort of made sense.

It'd been a month since we were all last together, and Caleb still hadn't returned from his travels up north. James had come to visit me, and here we walked near my house, along the path behind the industrial estate. We were heading towards a street closer to the train station that hosted a coffee shop.

James had returned to his interest in thinking deeply, unafraid of going mad, and this led to some deep conversations over our time of knowing each other. But lately, it had taken a serious turn. Instead of just concepts, we were discussing reality, and feeling the full force of the ideas as we applied them to our real lives.

"If the things we see aren't the thing itself," he continued, "I mean, if the colours we see aren't physically in the world, and there are only waves of electromagnetic radiation, then what is the experience of something?"

"Some sort of hallucination?"

"Yeah and it means they only exist in the mind... we've established this. What I wonder is; what is that made from?"

"What are dreams made of?"

As we neared the part of the path where the poppies once grew, we noticed ahead was a familiar face. I couldn't remember where I had seen him, and then as we got closer, and I saw his blonde dread locks, I remembered he was the one who also harvested the poppies I planted.

He was throwing more seeds through the fence to where the old crop was. He caught glimpse of us and waved out, excited to be showing us what he was doing.

"Good to see you again," he said, eyes droopy and tired with dark circles that signalled he wasn't taking care of himself. Despite his appearance though, he had a calm and welcoming energy. I could tell he was a nice person.

"Planting more I see?" I asked him rhetorically.

"Yeah, it's definitely cheaper than buying pills, it would be nice to have this resource be ready all year round."

"Do you use a lot of opiates?"

"They're my favourite, or at least they were. I mostly take them now to not feel sick."

I'd heard this before, that at first drugs like heroin feel warm and comfortable, but soon after regular use people take them just to feel normal and avoid withdrawal.

Had I encouraged him and done a bad thing by introducing this man to more of the drug he battled with? Or perhaps since the poppies were natural, close to being free and empowered him to not be reliant on dealers, I had done a good thing?

I questioned this for a long time. The morals confused me, although I settled on the fact that I could not control his actions or make decisions for him, and it was not my intention to introduce him. I felt I stood neutrally, and did neither good or bad.

I thought that for many things in life this seemed to be the case, that a thing itself is neither good or bad inherently, it is our intention and how we use it that is good or bad. Food can be both good for you and bad. Drugs can be medicine or poison. It's us who determines it.

After talking for some time with the man, we said goodbye and continued on our walk without getting his name.

"What was his name again?" James asked.

"I forgot to ask, but I'm sure we will see him again, he feels familiar in that sense."

"What do you mean?"

"You know when you meet someone, and they already feel familiar. Like you have met before in the future, or you know they play a part in your life before you really know how," I explained.

"Yeah I do get that sometimes, funny how that is." I was glad James understood.

We had reached the end of the path finally, and walked out into the open street at the end. There was the bridge that crossed the railway line to the left, and we walked underneath it towards a coffee shop on the other side.

How I longed for a coffee this morning. We had no plans for the day, and the coffee shop was the only destination I had in mind. We walked towards the entrance, opened the door, and inside it was empty, only occupied by the workers behind the counter.

I ordered a small cappuccino, and James opted for a mocha, and as we waited for our orders to be ready we sat by the window and watched the world slowly go by outside.

NINETEEN

It was seven thirty, still early, and so only the workers of society who I assumed started at eight o'clock walked by in their button up shirts and formal attire.

"We choose the life we live," I said to James. He noticed my observations when I said it and agreed.

"For some the life inside the confines of the mind is a safe one. The invisible structure society sets for us provides direction and comfort. And it's an experience as necessary as those who choose to live freely and create their own path."

I agreed. How could we judge, while we enjoyed the benefits of what society provided.

"I wonder how Caleb is," I said. He had come into my mind by what felt to be some random reason, spontaneously but from somewhere, and as I finished saying those words, I saw a familiar face walk past the cafe window.

"There is no way, that's him?" James exclaimed, and before he could walk too far past the cafe we got up from our seats and opened the door to call out.

"Caleb?!" We said. He stopped in his path and looked towards us, smiling widely with a genuine surprise.

"I thought I might run into you here!" He said to us.

"We literally had just said your name wondering where you might be. How strange," I told him.

"A perfect synchronicity, it means you are in flow," he said to us, "let's walk, I was heading to the station, the train leaves down the coast soon."

We walked again towards the bridge overpass, and up some stairs that led to the top, where we could cross it towards the station. And just as we walked down the stairs on the other side of the bridge to reach the platform, the train arrived, the doors opened, and without pause we smoothly walked on.

Just as we found our seats, the train doors closed, and we started travelling south towards James and Caleb's town.

We watched outside the windows at the passing infrastructure, until it led into green farm lands, rocky beaches, and dense bush. The mountains sat as a slower moving wallpaper at the back of the scenery, framing our vision of the world.

And after some time, we arrived at the station of the town where James and Caleb lived.

"How long have you been gone for now?" James asked Caleb.

"At least a month," Caleb said, "I remembered on my trip that I gave you something special. Do you still have the envelope I gave you?"

I had forgotten all about it, and it still remained unopened. Sure enough, I did have it on me. In my pocket was a destroyed envelope, I assumed it had been heavily impacted by the washing machine. How curious that I could carry something I had forgotten about.

I reached in and sifted through the ripped up pieces of paper to find a small plastic bag, and when I pulled it out of my pocket, it seemed to contain a yellow powder. How fortunate for the contents to survive.

"Do you know what that is?" Caleb asked, as we all stood around it observing it with curiosity. "Put it away and let's go back to mine, I'll show you."

Holding some sort of drug openly at the train station wasn't the smartest idea, and I realised when Caleb said this. I put it back into my pocket, and we began walking.

It was about an hour by foot to get to James and Caleb's house. We made our way towards the bridge that crossed the large river at the end of town, and walked across to the other side.

From there, we walked through the town, observing the people and buildings as we passed. It was a mostly silent journey, as we carried a feeling that something big was on the horizons of our timeline.

I watched as a man walked towards us, slow paced and bearded. 'Enjoy,' I thought for some reason, and as I looked to him, he looked me in the eyes, and said "enjoy". How uncanny.

I could assume his intention was to say 'enjoy the walk,' but it was as if the universe was speaking to me with the message of "enjoy what is to come."

There was a familiar feeling in the aether, as if I had lived these moments before, and it was a core memory from my future.

"I feel something is coming. This all feels so familiar... uncanny."

"I feel the same," James said, as Caleb nodded in agreement.

We continued towards the park, across green grass and past intentionally placed trees, and when we reached the other side, it was a short walk up that road where we came to James and Caleb's house.

TWENTY

135

It was the same door I knocked on months earlier, when the smell of marijuana seeped through and I had consumed MDMA and cough syrup. How so much had happened in a short time; it felt as if it was years ago but yesterday.

We entered, and turned left down the hallway towards Caleb's room. His was the nicest in the house, with a king sized bed that had a carved wooden canopy extending like a roof over the top. The room was neatly laid out, cosy and had nothing out of order.

When inside, Caleb opened his drawer and reached in, taking out a glass pipe that had a bulb end. Typically used for methamphetamine, which I wanted to avoid ever doing, I had never used anything like it.

"This is my DMT pipe," he said, reassuring us that we weren't going to do meth. As he said that, it all started to make sense.

I reached into my pocket and took out the small ziplock bag and handed it to Caleb. He delicately scooped some of the powder with a small spoon onto a set of scales. He measured out fifty milligrams, and placed it into the end bulb of the pipe.

He handed the pipe to me, and I sat on the bed in a position ready to lay down.

"You want to lightly heat the bottom of the bulb, enough to vaporise the powder but not to burn it. When you do this, inhale deeply. It may get to a point where it's difficult to want to take more, but you will need courage to continue."

I nodded, with a respect for what I was about to do.

I began to lightly heat the bottom of the bulb with a lighter, and I began to see vapour build in the end.

I inhaled. It was an oddly familiar taste and smell. Very strong, it reminded me of age.

I inhaled deeply, as much as I could, and held my breath. I could feel it sitting in my lungs, and then after five to ten seconds, I felt it enter my body. It was an absorption I had never felt before. I could feel its presence leave my lungs and occupy my entire being, like being submerged, but not in water.

A buzzing began generating in the centre of my head, and soon encompassed the entire room. "Zzzzzzz schzzzzz schwzzzzzzz," I could feel the vibration in everything, accelerating at an uncomfortable pace.

"Woahhhhhhhh my," I said as I exhaled, and was reminded by Caleb to finish what was in the pipe.

I heated the bulb once again, and inhaled deeply once more. Again I felt it enter my whole being from my lungs.

The vibration increased, and the world morphed around me. It shifted as if I could see the room through different perceptions. Shadows faded from light to dark, and colours were vibrant and changing in irregular yet intelligent ways.

I laid back and closed my eyes, and a green looking overlay of moving snake-like patterns encompassed my vision. In the distance, I could see a spherical orb move closer, and I could hear a celebration approaching.

And as it reached close enough for me to gain clarity on it, I heard a typically joyful and choreographed yet genuine "hooray!!!" I felt a child once again, being introduced and welcomed into a place with such love and excitement. I felt I was home, and I was back and had returned, it was just that I had forgotten I had been here before.

"I remember this."

"We love you! We are so glad you are here!" I heard from some other presence as clapping surrounded me. Communication was an understanding, and I could see and experience the sounds of their words and intentions in more ways than just hearing. I knew what they were communicating, and they knew what I was communicating. It was an understanding - a kind of connection deeper and more personal than any other I had experienced.

This sphere visually was a world, immersive so much that it encapsulated me, and contained non-physical objects that transformed themselves unto and onto themselves. They were not static shapes, but whole timelines of themselves, where I could see their beginning and ending, and in all angles, all at once. They were more than three dimensional in this way, and filled with vibrancy and colour.

Everything seemed to be a sort of cartoon, yet felt more real than reality itself. It felt like a more fundamental base reality. One that was limitless, and infinitely creative. And as I watched as these objects transformed onto themselves, as the whole world I was in also did, when everything returned to its original place again, I got a feeling of Deja vu.

This four dimensional world was repeating as I experienced its full shape, and as I looked around I noticed that those that lived there that I could see seemed to be elf-like creatures. Almost appearing as a leprechaun, with a small triangular pointed hat, one approached me, as real as anything I had seen in my life. I was in awe at its realness, and felt a rush as I was comprehending what I was experiencing.

"Yeah, I'm real," it said as it nodded. I could understand it talking to me without words, and it could understand my thoughts. Its hands appeared as separate from it, with emotive gestures that fitted what it wanted to say.

"Follow me," it said, as its hand gestured for me to come forward. I trusted it and followed.

And as I did, we approached a door that was hiding behind the transforming objects of the world. It appeared as a typical door with a green lit up exit sign above it. It was cartoonishly simple yet realistic and not transforming like everything else.

The door opened and we entered, and on the other side was an open space, with the sphere in the distance once again. And as we approached the sphere, it gained clarity again, and I heard once more, "hoorayyy!!" with more clapping and celebration and love.

And when I found myself in that same place encapsulated by the sphere again, and in the presence of self-transforming and vibrant shapes that I find it difficult to describe, we made our way towards and behind them to the same door with the exit sign above.

We entered once more, and again I saw the open space with the sphere in the distance. Faster this time, we approached. "Hoorrayyyy!!" clapping and cheering filled my heart with love, excitement and embrace. More quickly again we continued behind the shapes, towards the door, and through into the open space.

Things were speeding up, but as they did, the elf remained with me, which was a comfort. This journey continued as a cycle, with ever increasing speed. This sphere seemed to be a higher dimensional shape in which I was repeating through it over and over, and this gave me a strong feeling of Deja vu each time I returned to the beginning.

And as the repetition through this experience continued to increase in speed, I thought to myself, and the elf could hear it as a question, "what is the meaning? What is this place?"

In that moment, a profound insight became available to me.

"Your world is made of mine. All that exists are ideas, and imagination, and from this your world can be constructed."

And just as this insight was absorbed by my consciousness, the ever accelerating experience of the sphere, the hooray, and the door had become so fast that it was as if I had lifted from its plane, and could see it as one whole shape. And this shape, as the sphere, retreated away from me just as it had approached in the beginning.

I watched it become smaller in my vision, and understood that the time had come to leave. And when it finally disappeared into the vanishing point in the distance, I could feel my body again, and the bed beneath me.

I opened my eyes slowly, in a relaxed state, and looked up at the wooden bed frame above.

Caleb and James were also sitting on the bed, watching to ensure I was okay. I smiled, and they smiled back. Things appeared the same, but there was a different perception of it all in my mind.

"Welcome back," Caleb said.

"Glad to be here. Thankyou for that," I said with true authenticity and impact. "Really, thankyou. I cannot believe that exists. There are no words."

"Sometimes to describe it is to take away from it. Just let it be for you," Caleb said.

I realise now that when I looked at things, they appeared less physical and softer. As detailed but less complicated, more holistic.

As I looked at the drawers, I could understand how the idea of the drawers preceded the physical construction of them. It was as if the imagination, and non-physical energy, was the base, which presented itself as atoms, wood, metal, and hard physical and 'real' things. This energy displays what I perceive, but isn't what it displays.

TWENTY ONE

James and Caleb had opted not to do DMT that day, and let the experience be what it was for me. Perhaps they would choose to do it at some point in the near future, and so I left the rest of it with Caleb, where he placed it in his drawer with his pipe.

I felt a sense of calmness and profundity in my aura. All my worries and feelings of unease had left me as I realised they were insignificant and meaningless in the larger framework of things, and mostly stemmed from my perception of a 'physical' and separated world.

If the universe is entirely mental, and made of something non-physical and indescribable, then it is all more connected and magical than I previously thought.

James made his way to the kitchen, where he filled the kettle and turned it on. As it made its way to a rumbling boil, he filled three cups with instant coffee, ready to be brought to life by hot water and milk.

We sat in the lounge room, the blinds open revealing a picturesque blue sky with light fluffs of clouds. The steam rose from the coffee with a white purity this time, as if the world was made of light.

www.ingramcontent.com/pod-product-compliance
Lightning Source LLC
Chambersburg PA
CBHW020340260626
47156CB00004B/1627